For Lulu and Charlie,
with love from Gigi—SW
For my principal, Mrs. Davis—JE

PENGUIN WORKSHOP
An imprint of Penguin Random House LLC, New York

First published simultaneously in paperback and hardcover in the United States of America
by Penguin Workshop, an imprint of Penguin Random House LLC, New York, 2022

Text copyright © 2022 by Sarah Weeks
Illustrations copyright © 2022 by Joey Ellis

Visit us online at penguinrandomhouse.com.

Library of Congress Cataloging-in-Publication Data is available.

Manufactured in China

ISBN 9780593226971 (hc)   10 9 8 7 6 5 4 3 2 1 TOPL

Blippo & Beep

by Sarah Weeks
illustrated by Joey Ellis

Penguin Workshop

CHAPTER ONE
Beep Tells a Joke

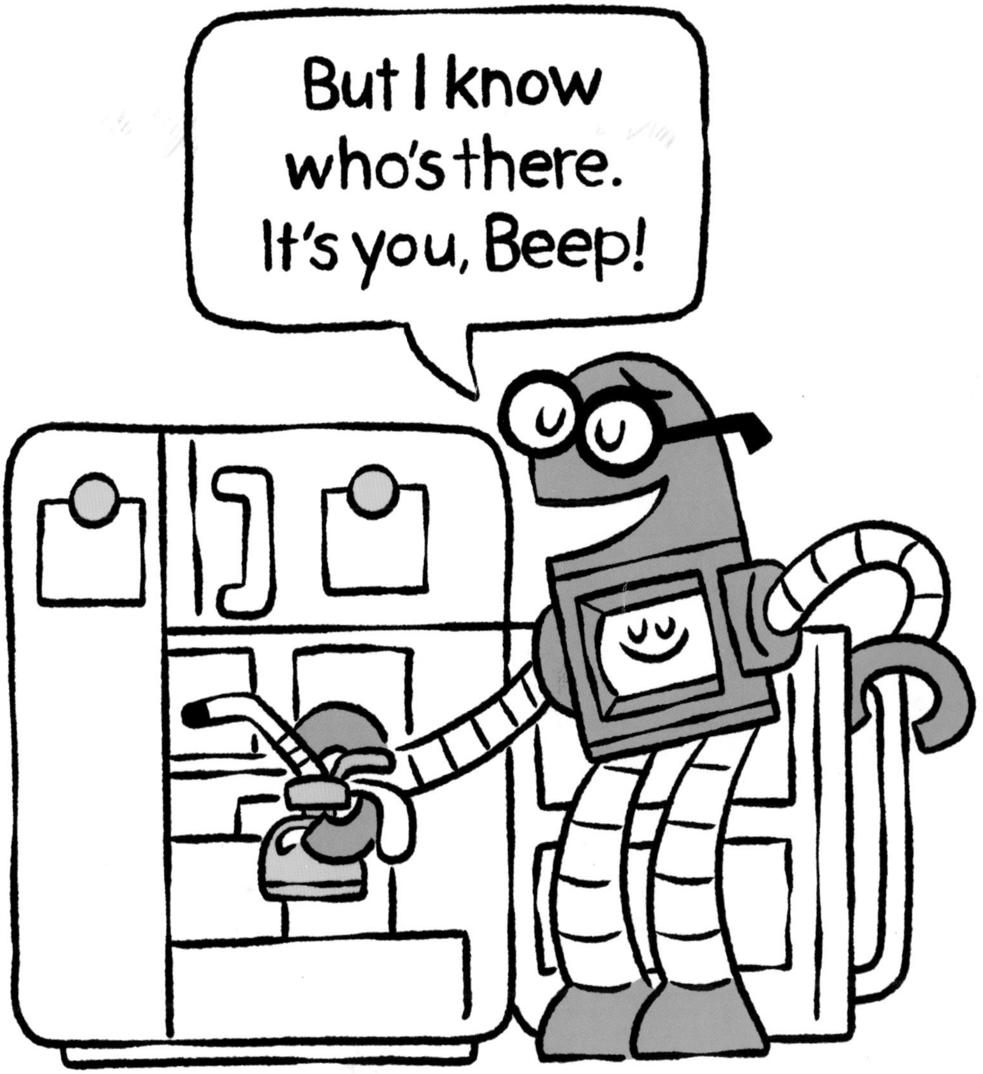
But I know who's there. It's you, Beep!

CHAPTER TWO

Blippo Tells a Joke

Do you want to hear a joke, Beep?

Is it a knock-knock joke?

What is **big** and **blue** and likes to eat cereal?

You?

CHAPTER THREE
Blippo Tells a New Joke

Let's make up a **new** joke!

44